I0700530

LYRA

LYRA

EMILY FRANCHINI

Cover design by Rachel Kelli

ISBN 979-8-9862328-0-5 (hardback)

ISBN 979-8-9862328-1-2 (paperback)

ISBN 979-8-9862328-2-9 (kindle)

ISBN 979-8-9862328-3-6 (ebook)

Dedicated to my loving husband, Brian.

Edited by Aly Owen
Brought together by Reedsy

HELP IS AVAILABLE

US National Suicide Prevention Lifeline: 800.273.8255
You may also call, text, or chat: 988

For TTY Users: Use your preferred relay service
or dial 711 then 1.800.273.8255

Prestamos servicios en inglés 1.800.273.8255
y en español 1.888.628.9454

Disaster Distress Helpline: 1.800.985.5990

See Appendix for more resources

CONTENTS

CHAPTER 1

SETTING THE STAGE

———

His name I will not tell.

An androgynous voice filled her head again. Lyra began to listen a bit more intently as she kept her eyes on the television. She was fixated on a blonde woman presenting the morning news. The lady had a most serious voice as she discussed shootings, presidential happenings, and world events. She could probably deliver obituaries and lottery winners in the same breath, and nobody would notice the change in topic.

For you may know him.

"His name...I will not tell. For I may know him," Lyra whispered to herself as anxiety and anticipation creeped into her heart. She hung onto the words for a moment, trying to decipher the meaning. It seemed quite literal—that the voice was simply trying to avoid telling a secret about a boy, since they used "him" as the pronoun. Lyra got up and turned off the TV. She was already bored with it, and the voice speaking between her ears made it hard to concentrate.

And I will become shy, because you know him.

She mused at the strange voice. The master of the voice was certainly entertaining to think that she would know this voice's secret crush. A wave of uncertainty coursed through her as she anticipated the next line. Would this be all the voice had to offer today?

For I am 15 and falling for him.

She sighed, both in relief and exasperation, as she heard the latest line from the voice. "You must be tortured," she whined. But the voice never noticed when she talked to it. The voice continued, and with it, the anticipation of where it would take her next.

Freeze time…time's not listening.

"Of course it isn't," Lyra rolled her eyes at the voice now. She almost turned on the TV again, but that noise would do her no good. The voice was always heard clearly, no matter what she was going through.

I long to be with him.

She grunted and shouted "Be with who?!" with no hopes of receiving any sort of answer from the voice. "Or whom," she muttered. She could never really tell if it was supposed to be who or whom in those questions.

She silently appreciated, as she often did, the fact that

she lived alone. Living with family was hard when the voices began to speak. They'd sent her to an inpatient facility a few times because of her outbursts during psychosis. It would usually start with Lyra's being moody and then wind up with a meltdown that just wouldn't stop. Death Spiraling, so to speak. Over the years, her relationship with her family had deteriorated from a lack of understanding and communication. She attributed it to the fact that her family wanted to pretend that they were a normal happy family. And Lyra just didn't fit the aesthetic.

It was particularly rough when these outbursts were triggered on Christmas Eve. Santa brought Lyra special mittens that attached to a belt the year that Lyra wouldn't stop picking at her skin. Lyra remembered the doctor gave her behavior the funny name of Dermatillomania. Her religious family shortened it to mania in their Facebook post seeking for thoughts and prayers.

When the voices spoke to her in public, she would listen, but become withdrawn. But then the anticipation of either silence or normalcy would overwhelm her. And when she was alone, she would sometimes speak back in hopes that the voices would go away or change their topic if she confronted them directly.

Lyra rolled up her sleeves and got up from the couch. It was time for her to be productive today, or so her anxiety thought. "You lazy bitch" floated around in her head as she meandered towards the kitchen and began to unload the dish washer.

I can't fall in love with some other guy.

It's not happening.

"You think that loving just him will increase your odds?" She snickered at the voice. The voice was neutral in general cadence. She grabbed a towel and began to wipe the dishes that still had droplets of water on them.

I still wonder if he thinks about me.

The music stops,

He lets go,

And my heart goes with him.

"What a heartbreaker he must be. WHOEVER HE IS!" Her voice was already getting sore from her shouting. "Or whomever," she whispered.

She continued to finish her dishes and then sat down, scrolling through the ever-depressing feeds of her social media. Heather had a baby. Sarah was graduating. Fiona was grabbing dinner with her beautiful family. Mike was checking out the bikes in season. Scroll scroll scroll…"And Lyra was hearing voices again," she murmured to herself.

It had been 30 minutes since the voice stopped. She wrote down the voice's words in her notebook and added a time stamp. Organization for the chaos is key to keeping it under wraps. Or at least, that is what the therapist said once, and it stuck ever since. She now had a small collection of notebooks filled with thoughts, therapy, and voices.

Lyra put a footnote on the page:

It seems that this voice was a teenage girl who was tormented because of a boy who doesn't know she exists. If she were a tangible person, I think she should forget about boys entirely. But alas, this voice is another forsaken figment of my imagination. Not one of the most inspiring voices I've heard. But, also not the more frightening ones either. I think I'll call this one Missy. Missy the lovestruck teen.

Lyra signed and dated the entry and then closed her notebook promptly. It was time to eat! She fumbled through the fridge for some of the food that she prepped for the week and grabbed a Tupperware full of spaghetti. She tossed it in the microwave and pressed the three- minute button. She grabbed her phone again and began to scroll.

It was 5pm. As she often did, Lyra ate in silence and enjoyed it. The spaghetti was especially delicious today. She looked up and saw the sun touch the hills. The light began to bronze, and the clouds were slowly streaked with blues and pinks and purples. It was as beautiful as a stained glass window in a Catholic church. She cracked her window open to let the cool breeze in. It smelled of pine and bonfires. She loved it when her neighbors burned their bonfire. She took a deep breath in and let the air fill her with something that resembled joy. Her anxiety and self-critic shortly followed behind it. "You should really get your own bonfire going and stop bumming off your neighbors."

She finished her dinner and tossed the Tupperware in the sink before grabbing her jacket and keys and locking up the house. She jumped into her Jeep and began to make the trek to work, which involved crawling down the winding roads to the main strip of the touristy town Hot Springs. She wasn't particularly excited to work since her episode with the voice. But she kept her schedule today. She might even see Lucy, her sister-in-law and boss. She turned into the parking lot of a boutique called The Little Stream and parked in her spot. She was glad nobody had already parked there. It would just be another sign that the universe hates her today.

She saw Lucy's silver truck in the back. Stuffing her keys into her pocket as she walked up to the store, she rang the bell. Lucy opened it with a warm smile painted on.

"Hey Lyra, come on in!"

"Hey Luce."

"Soooo tonight's shipment isn't here yet—I'm thinking they probably got stuck somewhere in central Arkansas…you know how that big city traffic is," Lucy said as she led Lyra to the office in the back of the store.

"Typical. They are always having issues. 130 seems to be always down due to construction."

"Yeah, I was hoping to get the new summer line here before the weekend. Spring break is almost here, and the customers are going to want summer clothes for their vacations coming up."

"Got to be ahead of the times?"

"Always, Lyra. Anyways, how was your evening?"

"It's good."

"Oh? Anything particularly interesting?"

"No."

Lucy sighed, and Lyra shrugged as she attempted to turtle into her body. The silence was deafening and made Lyra brace herself for another mental hit. "You are the worst sister-in-law ever" bounced in her head, which then sparked the next thought of "No doubt you are also the biggest disappointment to the family. I mean look at Lucy—successful, pretty, and everything that you aren't." Lyra grimaced and mirrored Lucy's sigh.

"Lyra…maybe you should take up a hobby."

Lyra forced a smile, "Maybe one day."

They said their goodbyes; Lucy was off to take care of her children and husband. Lyra felt more comfortable when she was alone anyway—that's one reason why she worked evenings. She got right to cleaning up the shop, hoping that the shipment would arrive for Lucy. They already had the shop ready to receive it, and she was prepared to dress the store.

CHAPTER 2

THE DARKNESS

———

Surrounded by darkness in a lonely world.

The voice was deep, dark, and foreboding. Their voice sounded absolute and lingered in Lyra's mind. She was at home now, watching a movie on a streaming channel while in full comfy clothes, and sighed softly as she felt the heaviness of the voice. Her heart felt heavy at the "lonely world" bit, but she tried to pay more attention to the movie that danced in front of her eyes.

Her feelings been abused again and again.

She latched onto the word "abused," and her stomach started to feel queasy. Her mind immediately jumped to memories of when her mom would tell her that she was being silly and how she wished that the doctor would prescribe stronger meds to make Lyra normal. She could hear her mom saying "You were such a good girl when you were little. What happened?" As if the environment was never a factor.

Lyra got up and paced around until her thoughts reminded her that she was going to try to get ginger tea. She pulled out the k-pod of coffee she had left in the Keurig from earlier and placed a new mug under the spout.

She attempted to get lost in the ritual of tea making: push the power button, grab a tea bag, wait for it to steep. Another memory shot out, and her mother's voice clouded the wafting smell of ginger: "You're being unreasonable, Lyra. These voices are all just in your head. That imagination of yours is just too wild—you need to get your head out of the clouds."

"You need to get your head out of the clouds," Lyra repeated out loud as she grabbed the tea timer and turned it upside down. She slowly shook her head, grabbed the honey, and let it drizzle into the clouds of steam floating out of the mug. A deep sigh escaped her as her memories continued their path of unwelcome nostalgia. The front desk of an inpatient facility. Lyra crying and screaming that she didn't want to go. Her mother screaming back that she had enough and that Lyra needed the help as she frantically tried to complete the intake forms. If only embarrassment could kill…a tear spilled onto her cheek as she silently wished that it had.

She feels as if there's no end.

The tears kept falling as Lyra pulled the tea bag out

and let it drop into the trash can. "Please stop," she warbled. "Please just stop."

She cries and cries,
day by day,
night by night.

She thought about all the times she had cried herself to sleep just like this. She would agonize over every stupid word she said or how dumb she looked in her secondhand clothes that never really fit. "You're so ugly" and "You're so stupid" would haunt her on a loop each night. Today's events just further proved those fears were true.

The darkness grows, and her heart is black.

She remembered when the nurses at the facility would grab her wrists and tie her arms down in cotton tie restraints while another would inject her with drugs. She would struggle and scream at them, but they would always just inject and talk over her shouts to explain the need of the drug and the care they are trying to provide. It just didn't matter to Lyra. She didn't want the drugs, but even if it felt like an infringement on her freedoms and rights, she wasn't able to have a say in her care since her mother consented to treatment on her behalf. Lyra was especially terrified when they gave her sedatives. One second she would be trying to get out of the restraints, nearly hurting herself, and then, almost like magic, her body would begin to float. The nurses became shadows, and her head would sink back into the pillows. All the tension would just melt away, and it became even harder to concentrate. Help? Did she ask for help, or did she imagine that?

Nobody cares.

Then why should she matter or care?

The voice was right...Lyra didn't matter. Nobody cared about her. Nobody cared to check on her. Nobody cared about her opinions, her taste in music, her love for silence. Nobody cared. Period.

A flash from the voices came in perfect clarity. She saw a gun in her hand. She jumped and threw it down. She heard a crash and realized that her ceramic mug was smashed instead of the gun that she just had in her hand. She cried and began to scream as she put her hands to her ears to try to block out the voices' words and images."I'm so stupid," she moaned.

Maybe you shouldn't be alive anymore.

"JUST SHUT UP!" She screamed back.

She saw another image of two guns in her hands, and her kitchen became a hallway. She saw lockers, and in the corner of her eye, a cafeteria. She was at an intersection where there were doors with windows. She heard the cries of children as they ran away from her. She then heard shots and felt the kick of the gun. A child fell. She killed him.

She screamed louder and began to choke from her sobs. "GO AWAY" she screamed. "Go...away...!"

Her heart is as black as coal.

The images stopped, and she became aware that she was in her kitchen. Her hiccupping started to subside as she surveyed the damaged mug on her tile floor. Death was present. She pushed her forehead into her knees. Her face was burning. "Please stop...I can't take it anymore." Her throat felt like sandpaper.

Am I going to be important to anyone? No one hears her. No one answers.

"Please…I. Beg. Of. You," she whispered as she rocked herself back and forth with her frustration.

How can I live.

I only hurt people.

She felt the rise of a new wave of tears and tried to push the memories and false memories into her subconscious. A sudden flash of nausea and dizziness overwhelmed her until she crawled to her bathroom to puke. "Please… Please," she pleaded weakly into the toilet.

She flushed the mess and limped slowly to her bed that wasn't much of a bed while clutching her stomach. It was two mattresses stacked on top of each other. She sunk into her mattresses slowly so she didn't rock the momentary truce she had with her gut.

As she closed her eyes, sleep arrived graciously quickly.

CHAPTER 3

SILENCE

———

Lyra woke up feeling a bit achy. She didn't want to remember what happened last night and did her best to push the memories far beneath the waters of her subconscious. But doing that just made it circle back with even more ferocity. She sighed, "If I tell you not to think about a white elephant, you will think about a white elephant."

She slid off her bed and mulled over what day it was. Perhaps it was Saturday. She stifled a yawn as she slid on leggings and slipped her feet into slippers. She checked her phone and confirmed that it was Saturday. And she had six hours until she had to be at work. Thankfully she wasn't wakened by knocking or endless phone calls from Lucy or Lyra's brother, Henry. Henry was not as thoughtful as

Lucy. At least Lucy usually brought bagels.

She made her way into the kitchen and almost stepped on the remains of her mug. She sighed again as she grabbed the broom and cleaned it up. She was fond of her mugs. She made a mental note to shop online for a replacement…if she could find a sort of replacement. Perhaps she would find a better one instead and make new memories.

Her one-bedroom house wasn't much. But it was all she could afford on the wages she earned from her job with Lucy. It had a small kitchen, a bedroom, a bathroom, and a dining or living room area. Lyra had furnished it with things she found at some of the secondhand shops around town. Every piece of furniture had a different color and texture that was close to matching, but never quite did. However mismatched it may seem, it was still functional. Her home felt like it truly represented her in a way.

The voices were quiet this morning as she ate her breakfast in blessed silence. She cracked a window and heard the chirps of birds that were pecking at the ground for whatever worms or bugs that were out and about this season. They were probably heading home from their winter migrations.

Lyra cleaned her breakfast away and began to do some chores that she meant to get around to. Dusting. Sorting mail. Anything to keep her mind busy. "The devil finds work for idle minds," Lyra mimicked her mother.

She started looking around the house for things to put with her clothes in the laundry. She checked her blankets for any messes she might have created on them from eating in them. She checked the bathroom to make sure she didn't leave any clothes near the shower and grabbed the towels. She deserved clean bath towels. She then made her way to her washer and dumped everything in there, not mentally wanting to separate whites from colors or warm washes from cold washes. She decided to wash everything cold and dumped the detergent in there without really measuring it. She then pushed it to a regular load and let it go.

"You really should separate them and wash them better." She rolled her eyes at this thought.

She then took the trash out and replaced the bag in the bin. It took a lot of energy for her to get that done, and it had been almost a week since she last took the trash out. Trash Jenga started to become a thing today. She then pulled out a Swiffer and started sweeping and mopping her floors. She looked up at the clock and saw that it was already 10am. She must have squandered an hour from chore responsibilities.

Lyra picked up a philosophy book and began re- reading it. The human mind never ceased to amaze her. Even when hers was as disordered as it was. She followed the life of Plato in this book, as he is very popular in Arkansas literature. Many of her schoolteachers would pull him into their curricula. She assumed it was because of the church-friendly material that he presented. Arkansas has a church on every corner, so it didn't surprise her when she made the connection. Lyra imagined that other regions prioritized different philosophers when it came to their own canons.

"Location, location, location," she murmured softly.

Lyra finished a few chapters before she felt achy from

sitting down. She got up and stretched. She began to feel lonely without the voices to keep her occupied. She almost missed them. Not all voices were sad or cruel. Some of them she liked. She wished more of the good voices would return to speak on topics of philosophy so they might have a conversation about it. But alas, no matter how hard she has tried, she can't seem to control them. Or not yet, as she was determined to at least manipulate them. Like one would manipulate dreams…if one had the capability to do so.

Nothing much more happened that afternoon. Time was slippery, but it was nice to have a day without the voices, even if she missed them.

She headed to work and received in the shipment that Lucy was waiting on. The driver gave some spiel about how he got lost in Colorado, which had set him back a day. Lyra knew that Lucy was going to call and complain. But that is all Lucy could really do. She only had one distributor.

The night was also very uneventful. Lyra thanked her lucky stars and proceeded to do boring, yet normal processes for the rest of her shift. Lyra managed to smile at her work at the end of the night. And that is very rare indeed.

CHAPTER 4

THE STORM

Lyra had a moment of peace as she woke up on Sunday. She knew immediately that it wouldn't last for long, and the voices were going to return to torment her again.

Lovely lilies sitting there on the window ledge.

Lyra froze with angst. The voice sung each syllable with careful enunciation.

How can you sit there so beautiful when there is so much dread?

Lyra felt her heartbeat began to pitter patter. She looked at the clock. It boldly showed her that it was 5am. Her body was on the edge as she laid in bed. Lyra clutched the sheets to her body and pushed a pillow over her head, hoping it would block the sound of the voice.

I want to die but can't.

Lyra felt time slow to a pause. She hated when the voices spoke about or showed her images of suicides or murders. A wave of nausea dropped over her. The familiar call of the void pulled at her to commit suicide herself.

The images followed.

In one she grabbed a knife from the kitchen and plunged it into her wrist. In the next she was on the top of a cliff with nothing to prevent her from crashing into the sharp rocks below. She jumped. In another she crashed her own jeep into a train. She began to groan.

"You know where the knives are," her thoughts whispered.

"Stop it," she returned.

Lovely lilies what is your secret?

Tell me so…

The images subsided as the voice cut through Lyra's thoughts, showing her images of lilies on a window ledge and a young woman talking to them as she laid her head down next to them. "Tell me so," Lyra repeated. She imagined this voice could belong to this young woman. The vibe seemed nurturing. But as she focused on this mental image, the face was always blurry or hers.

I desperately pleaded to the creator to take my life away.

To let me die and make the sadness go away.

The image switched to the young woman crying hard. Lyra couldn't help but cry with her.

"Please…just go away!" she screamed. Lyra suddenly knew who she was. Her face was still blurry, but the feeling of recognition left her cold. She was looking at her childhood friend a bit grown up.

"You're a terrible friend for not checking on me." Lyra felt Tia's glare as her voice interrupted the original voice.

"I…I'm sorry Tia."

All I want in life is to rot in the ground.

Lyra kicked the covers off, "NO. YOU. DON'T. YOU! GO AWAY," she growled into the empty house.

I was free when I found the secret of the lilies.

They lifted my heart.

Lyra paused her tirade for a second. The voice seemed hopeful that there was something in life to look forward to. A secret of some sort that was shared between them and the lilies.

She felt compelled to get out of bed and purchase or find some flowers for her own window ledge. She vaguely remembered reading something that said having fresh flowers helped bring joy into households.

Lyra sat up and crossed her legs. "Indian style," she remembered, her brain pushing a memory of a kindergartner Lyra being told to sit Indian style in her classroom. She closed her eyes and exhaled everything out of her lungs. She began to think of all the bad thoughts and voices leaving her as she pushed all the breath out of her body. She then pursed her lips together and inhaled through her nose. "Breathe in the good, exhale the bad." She exhaled through her nose. She then put her left hand on her stomach and her right hand on her chest and inhaled deeply once again through her nose, making sure her stomach rose instead of her chest. After her next exhale, she began inhaling on the count of one...two...three. Then four on the next breath. And so on. She soon opened her eyes and evaluated each body part to see if there was any pain. She then opened her mouth to let a yawn escape. Breathing exercises always made her yawn. For an exercise that was supposed to increase oxygen flow, why did it always make her feel like she lacked it?

Her eyes stung a little from crying. She grabbed a Kleenex, relieved her nose, and tossed the tissue in the garbage can next to her side table.

"Lilies..." She tasted the words.

She began to research lilies on her phone. They were gorgeous flowers with various lower classifications. She was drawn to the Easter lily. She noticed that sometimes there were pink colors in the middle. She liked those best. Lots of flower shops sold them cheaply—perhaps they were easy to grow.

She investigated the symbolism of the lily in different cultures until she was too tired to keep her eyes open. She fell asleep soon with her phone on her chest.

"Lilies," Lyra murmured in her sleep.

CHAPTER 5

FEAR ITSELF

Lyra opened her eyes again and rolled over to her phone. It was 9am on Sunday. She lost an entire day to the events of yesterday. She felt achy and more tired now. It felt as if a weight was pressing on her chest.

She rolled out of bed and made her way into the kitchen. She reminded herself that she needed a new coffee mug to replace the old one. She grabbed another mug from the cabinet and made some coffee in the sweet silence of the morning. While waiting for the brew, she cracked open a window and let the spring breeze pass through the kitchen, filling it up with humidity. Arkansas seemed to have a specialty for humid weather. She could feel the stickiness on her skin and her hair beginning to frizz.

She poured cream and sugar into her coffee and drank it while anxiously awaiting the next voice. She looked around for the voice here and there. Paranoid that what she saw wasn't her full reality. Perhaps it was. Nothing moved, and it made her uncomfortable.

She quickly scanned the room and picked five things that she could see to try to ground herself: coffee pot, mug, honey, table, chair. She then picked four things that she could feel: spring breeze, cool floor tiles, fluffy hoodie, and the tickle of her hair brushing the nape of her neck. She picked three things she could hear: the birds chirping, the buzz of the AC unit, and the sound of her breath. Then two things she could smell as she took a deep breath in: coffee and honeysuckle. Then one good thing about herself: "I make an excellent cup of coffee."

She finished her coffee quickly. And then she began to go about her day in cleaning and sorting through things that attached to older memories. She began with her books. Her collection of books involved some of her dearest friends. Her first love, *Artemis Fowl* by Eoin Colfer. Several books she had to read for school: *Lord of the Flies*, *The Color Purple*, *Anthem*, and *Romeo and Juliet*. A few old college books she had grown attached to. She probably would never use them again, but she didn't want to part with the hundreds of dollars spent on paper that was deemed worthless as soon as the next edition was printed. She slid a paper towel over the shelf to remove the layer of dust. A bit lifted into her nose, and she sneezed. "Bless you." She meticulously cleared the dust from every shelf and repeated the process to remove any residual bits.

Being around these books made her think of summer vacation and being able to read as much as she wanted every day. Her mom didn't mind because it kept her out of trouble and she was advancing her reading skills. Lyra was only disturbed for dinner time or if there were any family events, like going to the movies. Lyra missed those lazy, peaceful summer days.

Lyra switched her attention to a box that her parents dropped off. It had been taking up a sizable portion of the living room table for a week or two.

"You're lazy for not taking care of this last week."

"You don't really want to do this. You can go work with something else."

Lyra pushed through her thoughts as she pawed through the items in the box. Some of them were old clothes that she couldn't fit in anymore. There were also a few books, long forgotten. One was *The Golden Compass*. The name caught her eye as she read the book reviews on its back cover. She had nearly forgotten about this one. Her mom saw the name and bought it for her, though she would later regret that moment of generosity once the Christian community rejected the content of the book. Lyra chuckled. She loved the book anyways and begged for her mom to purchase the next few books, but her mother declined and even requested to burn the first book. Lyra had been in tears and hid the book. She was surprised this book had been returned to her instead of burned finally like her mom had wanted. Did her mom forget? Or did she not care?

Lyra shook her head to end that line of thought and continued to work through the box and take keeper items to their new resting places. The items she didn't want to keep, she tossed to the garbage can. She resisted the urge to take them to Goodwill. She didn't think anyone would want her things. They were so old fashioned and in terrible condition. She hoped she made the right decision.

"But someone could have used that."

Lyra closed her eyes and moved away from the garbage and back to her bedroom. She left the light off but flipped on the TV.

She was glad that all day and all evening she had mostly escaped the voices other than the negative automatic thoughts. She got ready for work and left the house in paranoia that a voice might visit her in the jeep or at work. Her chest felt a little tight, and her thoughts were bouncing around too quickly for them to land. She couldn't really focus on driving, so she threw the Jeep in park and glanced around. There was a pressure on her earlier peace of mind that she could not shake. Her ability to focus on anything was fading quickly.

But the voices didn't come.

She slowly made her way to the shop and was immediately confronted by Lucy.

"I didn't see you at church yesterday, Lyra."

Lyra had totally forgotten about the lost day yesterday, and a new wave of uneasiness overwhelmed her. If there is a God…please just let her drop this. "I'm sorry, Lucy. I couldn't sleep Saturday night and woke up very late."

"Excuses, excuses! The pastor was asking about you. I even texted you to ask you where you were at! You didn't even reply to me today."

Lyra picked up her phone and apologized. There was the text…all five of them. "I'm sorry Lucy, I got caught up in cleaning my house. I barely looked at my phone." Lyra hoped this deflection would work. "You know Lucy is going to see right through your bullshit Lyra." Lyra cringed at this voice.

"You know your relationship with the Lord is very important. You should come every Sunday to rejuvenate and develop that relationship so that the bond between you and the Lord is strong. And perhaps he can cure you!"

Lyra winced. She was annoyed that Lucy continued to invite her into church. The people there felt like they expected a lot out of Lyra, and Lyra doubted that Lucy would understand or truly hear her concerns. So, Lyra took a defensive approach to things and used her poor sleep schedule as an excuse.

Lyra shrugged, and successfully redirected the conversation to work duties. The shop was a small boutique, and the other employees worked part-time, but Lyra was used to working full-time with Lucy. Lucy was grateful to have her and gave her many partnership picks, like the title of business partner. But Lyra never saw herself as much of a business partner. She was more of a stock employee and whatever else Lucy needed Lyra to do…so long as it didn't involve talking to customers. Lyra was not as personable as Lucy. Lucy regretted having Lyra try to be a cashier after a regular tried to return a dress for not being a forever dress. Lyra had refused a return based on Lucy's policies and had insisted that she could not complete the return. But she didn't know Lucy had bent her rules to certain customers who provided repeat business. The regular had vowed never to return to the business again and had left a nasty Yelp review. Lyra's name was slandered just as much as Lucy's was. And ever since, Lyra had been relieved of all cashier duties.

Lucy left after she provided thorough instructions about the displays and chores that needed to be done. The night was uneventful, other then the brooding paranoia that something would happen. Or that she was being watched. That weight still sat on her chest. She checked the parking lot several times, but she was the only jeep in the lot. A sheriff would pass by here and there as he patrolled the area, but other than that, nobody was awake at the 10pm hour…usually.

Lyra felt pressured to finish as quickly as possible and get home. Her safety was at risk. She continued to look outside the window and keep out of sight. She even turned the lights off and worked in the dark and silence to prevent anyone lurking outside from seeing her activity in the building. She rushed her job. She took a second to look over it and just panicked. She had to get out of there even though it wasn't to Lucy's standard of order.

Lyra hastily locked the door and hurried to her Jeep. Her heart rate was up, and her calming breathing exercises were forgotten as she raced home, also forgetting that there was a sheriff out and about trying to capture people excessively speeding. She threw it her Jeep in reverse and squealed out of the parking lot. She glanced down at the Jeep's clock, and it revealed it was just a few minutes past midnight. Her heart rate was still up as she sped home. She took every curve tight, feeling the Jeep get pushed to the limit. She wished she could teleport home. Her frustration echoed into her driving as she continued to speed. Luckily nobody was out on the road to witness this paranoia- fueled drive. She finally could see her house, and relief seeped in as she turned into her driveway. But the paranoia continued to cloud her spirit.

She raced into her house and shut the door behind her, as if the voices were monsters trying to chase her home.

I walk in that long, dark corridor.

No light, not even a trace of sound.

"THERE THEY ARE! I told you that you cannot escape them!" She knew they would be here. She was caught, and the guilt of being captured by a voice sunk into her gut, making her even more distraught.

"I don't NEED this today!" She growled as she let out a sob and sunk into a ball in her hallway.

"But this is how it always is."

I knew not where I was going.

My clothes were torn and weathered.

She hugged herself tightly. Her breathing was even, but she shook uncontrollably.

My life was over.

I did not know what was next.

Was I forgotten, or even missed?

"I a-m-m-m Lyra," she stuttered, "I am-m-m not forgotten." Tears created a waterfall as she tried to fight it. "Am I missed?" She let out another sob.

My spirit was lost in a sea of tears.

Suddenly it was bright.

There was that hope again. It must be a false hope, though. Lyra couldn't trust this voice or the comfort that it tried to give her."I am Lyra." She repeated the affirmation, trying to ground herself.

I saw the light.

I knew I was in heaven.

But I was not ready.

Despair overwhelmed her again; the voice hadn't passed. The voice from earlier was suicidal, and this one was already dead. Perhaps they were the same voice. They had similar tones when it came to the sound of the androgynous voice, but their vibes were different. Lyra took a deep breath and tried to sort through all of the mixed emotions. It was internal whiplash.

There was a mirror.

I looked again, for I was beautiful at last.

I cried, for I was home.

Lyra felt her core quiver as she wiped her face. The voice finally seemed to be gone, and she slowly uncurled herself and picked up her keys from where she had thrown them. Between voices, paranoia, and general anxiety, her emotions took a severe toll on her health. Her shaking continued as she dropped the keys into a ceramic bowl.

Nobody truly understood how much energy it took to

resist the voices, and to act normal during times when the voices began to blend their memories, thoughts, and images with her own. She often had to rely on others to verify what was real and what was fake. But being isolated, she rarely had that option. Lucy was the only person she consistently interacted with. And even pretending to be human for her was exhausting.

She made some hot tea and sipped in silence on her bed. She knew the hot beverage would help with the shaking. She contemplated putting alcohol into the drink and drinking until she became numb. She was tired of processing—or rather, not processing—emotions that overwhelmed her.

Lyra rehashed the day. It started with the books and the chores. She cringed thinking about her rush job with the store. Her anxiety kicked her. "Lucy is going to yell at you next time she sees you. You should have done a better job. You're pretty worthless."

She sighed deeply at the word "worthless." Her mind reached for evidence of the worthlessness. It immediately brought her to a fight with her dad. He was yelling at her about how worthless she was because she didn't do any of her assigned chores for the day and had instead spent it reading and drawing. He was lecturing her on how she wouldn't amount to anything if she continued to discard responsibilities like this. Next she saw her mom kicking her out for not doing any of the chores. Which shifted into her brother's frustration with her inability to keep a job and contribute to their growing household. She felt herself drowning in feelings of failure and the lack of any support or even an inkling of understanding. She would have been homeless had it not been for Lucy's help. But she was a burden to Lucy…she had to be.

Lyra shut her eyes and pulled the covers over her head. She had had enough of this day. It was time to reset her body manually by sleeping. She took two Benadryl and four Melatonin gummies. Her mind continued to count all the ways she was a worthless human. Its review of evidence continued into her dreams.

CHAPTER 6

FLYING WITH HOPE

Lyra woke to the sun peeking through the blinds, casting its rays into her eyes. She winced when it touched her pupils.

"Nehhhum," she uttered as she pulled a pillow over her face. But the pillow bothered her, too. And soon she got tired of it all and just sat up, gazing around the room in weariness. She glanced at the clock. It was 8am.The sun rose around 7:20am this season. She sometimes wished for longer winters where the sun wouldn't rise till almost 8. Or maybe she should just purchase some dark curtains.

Lyra got up and moved to the kitchen to start her day with coffee and breakfast. She grabbed some bread and butter and made some toast. She felt a little better than she had been feeling as she took her coffee to the end of her driveway and gathered the mail and newspaper. She didn't expect anything other than bills or the occasional credit card advertisement. And as expected, she received just that. A water bill, an electric bill, and a credit card ad. She scoffed at the APR rate of 28 percent after a few months of 0 percent interest. She wondered what APR rate really meant. But her brain made the connection that this was the amount of interest the card would charge her for using it and failing to settle statements in full.

If I were to fly, what would it feel like?

A higher pitched voice pierced through her. She took a moment to reflect on rushing winds that would whip your face. Her palms became sweaty from the idea of being at a high height and looking down. Her grip on her coffee cup tightened as she raised it to her lips to take another swig.

Would I feel free?

Is flying like walking or running?

She started to think hard about this voice's questions as she walked towards her house. Would she feel free if she were capable of flying? Would it come naturally to her, like walking or running?

What would my wings look like, and where would they be attached?

Lyra smiled at this voice. It was very inquisitive. Lots of strange, but very interesting questions today. She imagined her young nephew or niece might fire off questions like this.

Would they be metal like an airplane? Or soft and fluffy like that of an angel?

Now, this was curious. Lyra never imagined wings made of steel or metal in general. She always imagined they would be soft and flexible like the wings of birds. But this voice compared soft wings to angels. That comparison piqued her curiosity even more because of all the religious talk in her life. If she were skeptical, she might think this were a sign. But she knew the voices made no particular sense.

If I were to fly, where would I go?

Lyra was thrilled by this question. "I'd go see Paris! And Egypt! And…well I don't know. I suppose I might stay home and keep them a secret, too. That might be the practical thing to do." She was inside her house now. She would pay bills shortly and then throw the advertisement in the fire.

Would I fly towards the stars and freeze in time?
Would I fly towards the sun and die anyway?
Who am I to fly?

"Who am I to fly?" she repeated. "That is certainly a great question. But the others? Freezing in time or into the sun?" She felt a weight placed over her heart. A seed of doubt was planted. So many questions. She bet Lucy would be exhausted, too, if her son, Xavier, asked all these questions within a short time.

The voice seemed to avoid more questions or provide any answers to the existing lingering questions. It puzzled her. It certainly didn't follow the pattern of the voices she had been receiving lately. She fetched her diary and wrote about the voices as she tried to remember them. She had forgotten to write about the mug breaking voice. Or the early morning one. Or the one that visited her right after work. And now this one, the inquisitive one.

"Ugh…should have done this after they were done. How stupid am I." She scribbled as much as she could. Her brain fog was heavy as she tried to remember what they said or how they made her feel. She summarized the previous few voices, but this one she wrote down the words a little more verbatim since it was so fresh. Her depression kicked her for being lazy and forgetful. "You're so stupid for not writing them down. You're never going to remember what they said ever again." Disappointment enveloped her.

She thought aloud as she wrote down her own answers to the voice's questions. "Hmm…flying with metal wings or soft wings? I suppose I would want to fly with soft wings if I had the choice. Less chance to poke myself with metal edges. And as to the where I would go…so many places. But I guess I'd have to eat and do other things as well."

"At least you were kind," she said definitively, as she tried to avoid thinking about the other voices. She preferred these types of inquisitive voices far more than the others. Anyone would if they were hearing voices and seeing things that aren't there. This voice was also kind enough not to give her any images that might go with its thoughts. She might have seen planes or sky diving or cliff diving.

Lyra pulled out the bills and her phone and started paying from online apps and the internet browsers. She was too cheap to buy a laptop or computer to pay these on. She consolidated her resources down to the essentials to make sure she didn't have to take on the responsibility of other devices. It sometimes bothered her when the apps didn't work or the words were too tiny on her phone. She wished the apps would get better. And she was hopeful that they would.

She then sighed as she looked at the clock and got dressed for work. She picked up her keys from the ceramic bowl and headed on back to the store. She drove more tamely, but the ghost of the paranoia episode haunted her as she made her way back to work. Her stomach began to feel uneasy as she remembered how reckless she drove. "You could have killed yourself." She felt guilt wash over her as she parked in her spot. The universe was being kind at least in that aspect—no one was parked there.

Guilt continued to fill her as she looked at the store. "Here we go," she murmured as she slid out of her Jeep and dragged herself into the store.

"LYRA! Did you really leave MY store like you did last night? Did you even see the mess you made?"

"I'm sorry—"

"NO! This is not acceptable. If you're going to be a partner, I need you to care just as much as I do about this store. And that includes the aesthetic! You HAVE to start caring and drop the excuses!" Lucy ran her hand through her hair in frustration and let out a little huff.

Lyra cast her eyes to the ground as she let shame, embarrassment, despair, depression, anxiety, and guilt suffocate her. She didn't know what to say, let alone what to do. "You're nothing but a burden. You see how she's talking to you." Lyra winced at her thoughts and insecurities. "I'll do better," she said to Lucy.

"You better." Lucy returned to her task of stocking the rack with new product.

Lyra took this moment to slip away and put her things down so that she could prepare for her shift. She then returned to help Lucy.

"Lucy, would you prefer metal or soft wings if you were given the option?"

"Pardon me?"

"If God were going to give you a pair of wings, would you prefer metal or feather wings?"

Lucy blinked at Lyra. "I think God would give me feather wings just like he'd have."

Lyra shrugged and carried on with work.

Lucy shook her head, "Honestly Lyra, that is such a ridiculous question. If you'd go to church more often and spend less time at home doing God knows what, you'd ask less of these questions and focus on what's really important. Like saving your soul and living your life in accordance with God. God is the answer, Lyra."

Lyra wished she had never asked Lucy about the wings. She could feel Lucy hovering over her to make sure she actually was going to do her job the right way this time. As soon as she confirmed that, Lucy left to go home to her husband and children. Lyra imagined her talking to Lyra's brother about the things Lyra had asked. She also imagined that she would receive a weird text from her brother asking her to go to church on Sunday. Maybe she shouldn't really talk to Lucy at all. Lucy seemed to be overly concerned when some of the voices led her to ask weird questions about life. She didn't understand that these types of questions were actually the more pleasant ones.

CHAPTER 7

THE COSMOS

———

Lyra was grateful for a silent morning filled with the ritual of coffee making. She made a mental note to get more coffee grounds, but also made another mental note of trying to write it down somewhere so she could actually remember the mental note. Tension washed over her as her mind transitioned to worrying about when the next voice would arrive. She felt the mental tug to look around. Someone or something had to be there. She kept pacing from the kitchen to her living room table, searching for a piece of paper. She then sat down and stared at her phone as she sipped her morning coffee.

"What will we do today?" She was still somewhat emotionally hungover from her week. The worthless feeling started to creep.

She went through her mental list of things to do. Bills were paid, Work was scheduled for later today. She started the list for groceries, so she could finish that. She wanted rice for a casserole, ramen, chips and salsa, hot pockets, lemonade, and almond milk. She didn't really like having a lot of food on hand, but she also didn't want to go out to the grocery store too often. It was exhausting. She pulled out a tub of leftover pasta and nuked it in the microwave. She put it on for four minutes. The perfect time for everything to be piping hot. Of course, she never let it fully cook for four minutes. She just listened to the food and watched it cook until she was satisfied with the food moving and shaking according to the temperature.

She ate in silence. She was sure that she was missing something in her to-do list. After she finished her food, she paced through the house, hoping to see something that she was supposed to do. She played a game of "touch whatever bothers you" and she found that she had left some jackets on the couch. She then turned to the bedroom and changed the sheets that had pools of drool stains. She then emptied the bathroom trash can and cleaned the shower. After all of that, she watched as the digital clock changed from 2:59 to 3pm.

The world is mine.

Lyra was puzzled by this voice. Its possession over an entire planet was a bit greedy. It seemed young in tone. She imagined that the voice might belong to an ambitious, power-driven teenager. Maybe they would be wearing a cape.

Nobody can take it from me.

The possession was sincere, but also came off as childish to Lyra. She decided to make a cup of tea just as a precaution for a panic attack. It had been a bad week, and as much as she was comforted by the voice doing its thing, she also hated the emotional toll a negative voice experience would create. This voice at least seemed docile enough. But she started to feel the pressure of anxiety. "You never get good voices," she thought. It shook its mental head at her.

I see flesh, delicate and tender.

Lyra tipped her head to the side and raised a brow. Flesh? Sounded almost like the owner of this voice was a bit on the macabre side of life. Maybe it would turn out to be a darker voice than she initially presumed it to be.

I wish to see a red stream.

"Your red blood."

She froze with fear as she looked at the freshly made tea. She swallowed the lump in her throat when she realized she was holding her breath. She began to breathe again, but her body was still frozen with fear. Her heartbeat picked up and she looked around to see where the voice was hiding, knowing full well that she would not find anyone. She bit her lip and watched the tea, grateful to herself for anticipating the need.

"We were right. Totes a negative voice. You'll never be lucky enough to catch a break. As per usual, you are weak."

"No..." Her reply to her inner saboteur was a weak one, but she was tired of letting it fill her with doubt.

The shine of the blade gives me shivers.

Lyra's brow furrowed as she pondered this last line from the voice. It didn't seem as gory as before. She took her cup of tea and sat down at the table as if she were going to have a conversation with the voice. She began to blow gently against the steam. But then she laid her head down on the table without taking a sip. She was tired.

It's a cruel world.

Lyra nodded. She agreed. The voice at least had some bit of common ground with her. She anticipated a burnt tongue if she were to drink her tea.

The seven deadly sins run amuck.

"Please be done," she sighed and said over and over. She didn't really want to engage with the religious tones of this voice.

She forced her head off the table and stood up, the anxiety and sadness from the voice slowing her movements. She was inundated with a series of flashbacks that included blades, her suicide attempts, and religious disagreements that got her in trouble. Her mind tried to flee the pain she inflicted on herself while her body responded by feeling weird at site of old injuries. Lyra could still see the scars, even though they were several years old. Her mind pushed back to several fights she had with Lucy and old school-mates. She probably lost each argument due to the level of virtue signaling they used as their debate strategy. Good people go to church, and church is full of good people with good morals. And if you don't go to church, you aren't a good person. "I'm a good person, too," she whispered to herself in the present.

When she made it to work eventually, Lucy was still pressuring Lyra about going to church. Lyra tried to shrug off the judgement and move on to more comfortable topics like work, but Lucy persisted.

"You ought to go to church with us on Sunday! We can even pick you up! Do you have anything to wear? Like a dress or skirt?"

Lyra looked sideways, "I don't own anything like that. I would stick out like a sore thumb." Lyra was more of a jeans and t-shirt kind of person. She had some slacks for when she went on interviews and a blazer. But she didn't really have any Sunday attire. Or at least nothing from her childhood of church attending that would fit her body anymore. By the time she was in her teens, she had been able to get out of going to church since her mental illness presented a challenge to her mom and dad.

"Nonsense! The Lord wouldn't care much for how his children attend church. Just wanted to keep the gossiping old ladies off your back." She gave a cheesy smile as she continued, "Just be up around 9am. I'll pick you up around 10 for the 10:30am session. Pastor Finch is looking forward to meeting you. I've told him all about you."

Lyra felt an overwhelming sense of dread and embarrassment. She bet that they talked about her in negative lights. "Lucy, I don't think I could go…what if I hear a voice and I go into another tantrum? I don't think I would be welcomed in such a place. I might even get sent to in-patient care if it's bad enough." Anxiety pushed out in the form of blunt verbal vomit.

Lucy grabbed her arm. "Then Pastor Finch will drive the devils out of you and bring you the voice of God."

Her look was dangerous and fierce. It finally hit her that Lucy wasn't offering to bring her to church to find God. And that angered Lyra. She wished she could sleep through the sermons. Perhaps the voices would be drowned by the dreams.

"If I go once, will you leave me be? Or is this going to be a regular thing?"

Lucy gawked. "It's going to be a regular thing Lyra. Your relationship with God is important."

"Maybe my relationship with God is private, unlike your relationship with the Ashton guy."

Lucy's eyes went wide with fear. "Don't you dare say a word about that to your brother."

Lyra looked her dead in the eye. "Don't drag me to church and I won't." Her heart was racing and her hands were shaking, but she let the anger keep her gaze steady.

Lucy slowly nodded in defeat and then changed the topic. Lyra was grateful for accidentally seeing her sister- in-law leave the storeroom late at night with another man on a night that Lyra forgot she had off. There was no mistaking that they had been going at it, with the used condom in the bathroom trash and the smell of sex permeating the store. It was repulsive to Lyra, but she couldn't be completely sure if it actually happened, or if she had imagined it, but based on Lucy's response now, she was pretty sure she was right. She was still terrified that Lucy could paint her affair as one of Lyra's delusions, but hopefully any resulting shame and embarrassment would prevent Lucy from using her mental illness against her. But that would be a tomorrow problem. For now, the religion discussion crisis was on hold again.

Lucy said her goodbyes with a little too much of a forced smile. Her higher pitched voice gave her away—she was apologetic and wished to escape Lyra's presence. Lyra was grateful that she left quickly so she could finally get to work.

The shop was perfect in Lyra's eyes as she locked it up and left it. It was her own version of an apology to Lucy. The night was very silent as she mulled over the hurt she inflicted on Lucy. And the hurt that Lucy inflicted on Lyra. It was a messy emotional night, but no tears would come. Maybe she had used the last of her reserves in the constant stress she's been under.

She drove home with a burned CD of her favorite hits playing."Havana ooh-na-na. He took me back to East Atlanta…la la la."

She pulled into the driveway safely and threw the jeep in park. The stars winked at her from outside the window. She smiled shyly at them before sulking into her home. She made sure everything was in its proper place before grabbing a hot pocket and nuking it for four minutes. She intently watched its bubble and pop process a little before pulling it out of the microwave. Hopefully most of the hot pocket was actually hot. She hated having to throw food back into the microwave.

She was satisfied with the hot pocket as she scrolled through Facebook. She liked a few of the posts and read through someone's rant about politics. Lyra wasn't really interested in politics, but she found it funny that some of her friends had some intense ideas about how the world should be run. She rolled her eyes when she got far enough into the thread to see the name calling. She then clicked her phone shut, put her plate in the sink, rinsed herself off in the shower, and changed into her oversized clothes and fluffy socks. She knew the evening air still held onto the chilly dregs of winter, but she enjoyed sleeping in the cold air.

She turned on the TV and began watching some documentaries about famous cases as she pulled out the Melatonin gummies. She took four and settled into the sheets, hoping her brain would finally shut down today. She was tired, both mentally and physically. Soon she began to drift and turned the TV off so it wouldn't wake her up. A deep sense of unsettled anxiety followed her into her dreams and continued to torment her the rest of the night.

CHAPTER 8

A CHANGE IN THE WIND

Lyra woke up groggy and a bit confused as to what day it was. She grabbed her phone and shook it to show the time and date. It revealed that it was Thursday. Her heart dropped. "I really don't want to go to work today," she muttered as her brain whined. She started to stress herself out with the thought of going into work. Her stomach began to gurgle in protest, too, so she texted Lucy: can I have the next two days off? I'm not feeling well.

Anxiety added to her uneasiness. "You're a terrible person. Lucy should totally fire you. You're probably going to get fired." Her phone buzzed.

"Of course you can have the day off! Hope you get some good rest. I'll see you tomorrow."

"Oh good, she bought it." Self-hatred sunk her back into bed. She was comfy for a second before her bladder decided to demand to see the toilet. "Every. Single. Time." Her mood shifted from self-hatred to anxious. "What are we going to do today? We aren't actually sick, so staying in bed shouldn't be an option." She thought for a moment, and then an automatic thought suggested tentatively "We could go out?"

"On a sick day?" she said to herself. "Won't we get fired for being out on the town?"

Her internal voice rolled its eyes at her. Her introverted part of her personality just wanted to stay home and watch re-runs of *Friends* and *Golden Girls*.

"Maybe we can go out for coffee with a friend?" "What friend?"

That stung. Most of her friends didn't really stick around after the first tantrum or two she showed them. She tended to scare them off with either her anxiety or the schizophrenia. Or hit them with both. Loneliness crept inside her. It seemed to be everywhere in the house. Maybe she did just need to get out before the house brought on another meltdown.

She headed to the kitchen to make coffee. She cracked the window while she waited for her Keurig to spit out the coffee into her awaiting cup. Lyra listened to the birds chip and sing their mating calls. The spring air felt pleasantly cool against her skin. She could taste honeysuckles in the air. Her nose was eager to go stick itself in a pile of them.

Today would definitely be the day that she would enjoy the town as a tourist of some sort. Even though she was a local. Lyra pawed through her closet to see which top would speak to her. She was feeling jeans with a nice top. She wanted something with sleeves and then found a nice sweater that wasn't too heavy if it decided to warm up, but also wasn't too lightweight if the temperature decided to drop. She wasn't really good at makeup or hair styling, so she kept it simple. She finished her outfit with a spritz of Calvin Klein's Woman.

Traffic was light as she maneuvered through the winding streets. She parked in the free parking behind a fountain and began to walk around the town looking for food and some peace.

Her loneliness began to creep on her again as she noticed several couples and families roaming the streets and shops. "Everyone thinks you're weird." She shook her head slightly at the thought. She imagined lots of people waiting for others would look alone for a minute…except she wouldn't be meeting anyone.

Lyra continued to walk through the small crowd, noticing people giving her a wide berth. "You're mean and ugly." The anxiety began to pour into her. "I'll just get food and go home…get food and then go home." The mantra was comforting and propelled her steps forward.

Lyra found a cute café and grabbed a bagel and a latte. She sat outside, nibbling slowly and enjoying the sunshine and slight humidity. Her nose quietly searching for that smell of the honeysuckle. She sunk into the chair, not really wanting to move now that she had some sort of purpose for being out.

He was just there.

Lyra looked around in quick movements. Most of the men in her immediate area were either with a woman or underage. She sighed softly in defeat. "I knew the voices would show up sometime. I'm not allowed to have any fun or time off. I don't deserve peace." She sat quietly and pulled up her phone to look as if she were reading something intensely. Tears of frustration lashed out at the girl-ish voice mixing with her internal dialogue.

I don't know how it started.

I was not really thinking.

Lyra took a deep breath and pushed it through her nose. The voice was very melodic, and she didn't have anything else going on, so she may as well suffer the defeat and listen in.

He is mine, and mine alone.

Lyra assumed this voice was talking about a boyfriend of some sort. She took a bigger bite of the bagel. It was delicious. Each bite was warm with flakes of cinnamon. She didn't know how long she had before she'd lose her appetite from nausea again, so she wanted to lean into her stress eating habits.

I've never felt this before.

It's an okay feeling.

Lyra wondered what sort of feeling was going through this voice's mind. Perhaps it was talking about desire? Lust?

Love? Fear? Excitement? It could be any number of emotions. At least the voice was private in talking about them. Sometimes the voices could be overly sensational.

He is my first boyfriend.

The voice seemed to be done with its dialogue. She waited a few more minutes to see if the voice would continue. In that time, she finished her bagel and latte and began to clean up the small crumbs that she made when eating. She tossed her trash in the bin and walked towards the different shops of the downtown area. She gave her shop a wide berth, but her fear of being fired and anxiety joined forces anyway. "Maybe you should go home." But then the loneliness of an empty house hit. For once she wasn't sure it was a blessing to have her own space.

She made her way through the fountains and tossed a coin for good luck. Or more specifically, for the voices to become more consistently kinder like these last couple.

Her focus shifted between not having gotten a firing text from Lucy, having the day off, eating that glorious bagel, and the smell of honeysuckle. She was so lost in the good things that she tuned out the rest of the world for a moment.

But then she practically ran into a young woman wearing a beanie.

"Oh, I'm terribly sorry!"

The young lady stood tall and smiled genuinely, "No worries. I don't mind being bumped by a beautiful woman such as yourself."

Lyra blushed a deep red. "Thank you, I suppose."

She surveyed Lyra, tipping her chin swiftly. "Maybe fate is trying to tell us something. Would you like to grab something to eat? Or trade numbers if you're too busy?"

She was bold. Lyra never imagined that she would attract a gorgeous woman like this one. All she could do was nod. The shock of being hit on by a woman rendered her speechless. She suddenly remembered to breathe and then mustered the courage to speak. "We can eat. I'm on vacation."

Forgetting that she actually called in sick from work and that she is definitely not on vacation. "You're an idiot, Lyra."

"Great! I saw a cute Italian place over there, if you don't mind Italian…?" She took Lyra's non-response as an answer and started to lead the way.

Lyra let herself be led by this beautiful creature into the crowd of people. Many pairs of eyes followed her. She imagined they were judging her for being with a girl, on a date. A DATE! WITH A GIRL! Lyra had had a total of two other dates in her past. And both had ended badly from the voices and their nasty habit of intervening with memories of things that they said never happened. But those other dates were men. She looked to the woman by her side. Perhaps a woman would be different…and then again, maybe not. "Remember, Lyra, the common denominator is you." She swallowed a cringe.

They entered a rustic brick building that looked like a two-story saloon. Stained glass windows trickled in colorful sunlight onto the fresh white linens. All the tables had a single rose and two candles for center pieces. The soft scent of garlic bread danced out of the kitchen and met Lyra and her companion's noses.

"Two please!" Destiny motioned to the waiter with two fingers. She clearly was comfortable with taking charge.

The waiter seated them and handed over menus before taking their drink order, which he promptly left to deliver to the waitress who would take the food order.

A million questions rolled in Lyra's head. "Why me. Why do you like me? Am I interesting? I thought I was intimidating." Finally, her mouth opened to release a statement. "I don't know your name."

"Oh! I'm so bad. I'm Destiny Starling. And you?"

"Lyra…Lyra Chester."

"It's nice to meet you, Lyra!" Destiny smiled. She was always smiling. "Where are you from?"

"I'm actually from this town. I took a few days off for some R&R. Where are you from?" A flood of anxiety washed over her as she waited for Destiny to answer. "Oh god I sounded stupid…so stupid. I just outed myself as not really on vacation. She's going to call you a liar, Lyra. Lying Lyra does it again."

Destiny flipped a menu page and answered, "I'm from the neighboring town Lonsdale."

"That's neat." Her inner critic was deafening. "Smooth Lyra…you nearly missed being called liar. Maybe you've been upgraded to a weirdo." Nervousness blended with anxiety and carved a half frown into her face as she tapped her toe to the ground to try to relieve some of the tension.

As they looked over their menus in silence, Lyra's stomach churned. By the time the waitress came to the table with the drink order, she wasn't sure she was hungry anymore.

"There you ladies are. Two waters. Are you ready to order?"

"I'm ready if you are, Lyra," Destiny said quickly.

"I guess I'm ready." She was definitely not ready. Her brain did not focus enough to make the decision. "I'll have the fettuccine and a Caesar salad." She hoped she made the right decision. She doubted that she wanted the fettuccine, but she also didn't really feel adventurous when it came to other foods on the menu.

The waitress turned to Destiny and Lyra watched as her company ordered flawlessly and without the slightest bit of doubt or hesitation.

"I'll have the pasta primavera with calamari."

"Excellent choice. Let me know if you ladies need anything else. I'll check on you in a few."

Lyra and Destiny murmured their thank you's before turning back to one another.

"So, Lyra, tell me about yourself."

Lyra pondered about as she let out a large, exasperated breath. "Where do I start…"

"At the beginning!"

Lyra laughed nervously. "Well, I'm 26-years-old. I live on my own. And I like the smell of honeysuckles."

Destiny smiled. She seemed so at ease even though she was talking with a total stranger. "Any hobbies?"

"Mug collecting." She could feel her mind rolling its eyes. "Lyra the mug collector. You really should get better and more interesting hobbies."

"That's cool. Are you an artist, or do you use the mugs for like coffee or tea?"

Lyra shrugged as she looked away. "I like coffee." How embarrassing. And uncomfortable. She didn't really like the spotlight on her. This conversation was going so poorly.

Destiny nodded. "Well, you already know I'm from Lonsdale. I have two beautiful mothers, and I guess you could say like mothers like daughter, because I also hope to fall in love with a woman one day. I work as a park ranger, and I raise dogs to search for people who are lost in the woods."

Lyra nodded. She wasn't particularly interested in sharing information. She regretted agreeing to lunch, but she hated conflict. "Look what you've gotten yourself into. You don't even know if you like women! And here you are on a date. Feel the discomfort!" She sighed audibly as she tried to fight with this voice and stuff it down further into the recesses of her mind.

"Is something wrong?" Lyra nodded.

"Is it me?"

Lyra shook her head adamantly. "I shouldn't have agreed to a date. Or whatever this is. I…I'm sorry." Lyra shuffled to get her things and leave before the waitress showed up to check on them. She was now terrified of what Destiny would say or do. Fear took over as she moved towards the door.

"What's wrong?" Destiny called after her. "I don't understand..." When Lyra looked back, she saw tears in Destiny's eyes. "...I just wanted to talk to a friendly face."

Lyra abruptly turned away and closed the door behind her before she ran into the crowds and towards her jeep. She imagined Destiny chasing her and demanding to know what is going on and why she was being rejected so suddenly. But when she had locked herself into the jeep and looked outside, no one was following her. She began to cry and collapse into a ball.

"I don't deserve to be loved," she moaned through her sobs. She let them flood her. When they started to die down, she grabbed some of the tissues in her glove compartment box. She felt the urgent need to go home. Fear and discomfort still held her whole body taut. She hurriedly fastened her seatbelt and almost forgot to turn the Jeep on before throwing it in reverse.

She managed to get home safely. Apart from almost getting side-swiped by a minivan of tourists. She yelled at them through the glass. She hoped they would all die. How dare they add even more fear to her day. She needed to get home. What if Destiny or the police were following her? By the time she got inside her house, she was convinced it was entirely possible to go to jail for leaving a date like she did.

She shut all the blinds, changed into pajamas, and curled up onto her bed. She turned on the TV for background noise. She turned her phone completely off in case the police, Destiny, or anyone else tried to call her. Her brain was still going a hundred miles a minute as it repeatedly analyzed her date frame by frame. "You're so embarrassing Lyra…can't even manage a date with a stranger." She had been on a date…with a woman…that she was attracted to? Was she? She was confused. But no matter what, her anxiety and fear were the only things she felt now.

She turned her phone back on. And then turned it off, as she reminded herself that the police might call her for her bad date skills. She pulled a pillow over her head.

"If there is a God…please take me now. Let me be the first to die of embarrassment."

CHAPTER 9

HANGOVER

Lyra's brain would not shut off or shut down. Hours went by with the gentle sound of the TV mixed with her internal dialogue's rehash of every frame of her day. She hoped Destiny was alright, but she knew that if she had continued to stay that Destiny would eventually see what sort of skeletons live in her closet.

"I don't even like myself. What chance would she have?"

She was having an emotional hangover. And she didn't want to do anything other than lie in bed and order a pizza. She liked not having to deal with humans much. She tipped in the checkout and asked them to ring the bell and leave the pizza on the welcome mat. The pizza place nearby knew that it was her, and usually complied. Rarely did they linger.

The pizza delivery individual came and did as instructed. Lyra watched through the blinds and waited until they had left again before she opened the door to get her food. She would make a poor secret agent. When she opened the box, she noticed someone had written "Here's a smile to cheer you up!" on the corner of the box. They even drew a smiley face, and a few employees had written small notes of encouragement. Lyra managed a small smile at their futile attempts to make her feel better. She grabbed a plate and put the rest of the large pizza in the fridge for later or tomorrow. She squeezed some ranch into a small ramekin bowl.

She climbed into her bed and tried to distract herself with a series. It was no use; her mind would wander back to Destiny. "You're probably going to be alone the rest of your life." Tears began to bubble at this thought. She wanted to believe she was a brave independent woman. But she also wondered what it would be like to have someone to share a home with. "I don't deserve love… nobody loves me." She looked down at her body, slouched over a greasy piece of pizza. She felt disgusted with herself.

Her evening became a cyclical battle between trying to watch scenes, relieving the earlier meeting with Destiny, and crying into her now congealed pizza. She was reminded of all her insecurities, from her aesthetic to her body to her social skills. Her inner saboteur pointed out every little thing that was wrong with her. Destiny would be better off without Lyra.

One day you'll wish you'd said something,
Something other than nothing.

"GO AWAY!" She was already overwhelmed, and this was her breaking point.

And I'll be dead by then.

"I SAID, GO AWAY!!" She screamed louder, creating a deep stab of pain in her throat.

I'll laugh at your misery when I'm in heaven.

Lyra threw her phone at the wall and flung her pillow at the TV. It rocked backward and hit the wall. "I said, SHUT. THE FUCK. UP. GODDAMMIT. LEAAAAAAVE. GOOOOOOOO. BEGOOOOOONE." Her moans deteriorated into incoherent sobs.

The voice did stop. But Lyra knew that it was because it was done, and not because she was done with it. She knew she should write about it in her journal, but she didn't have the energy. What was the point, anyway?

She turned off the TV and allowed herself to focus on crying. Gentle cries turned into sobs and then the coughing began. Her breathing became more labored by the amount of mucus pouring out of her nose. She tried to stem it with her sleeve. Her spirit was broken. A terrible date and then two voices. She couldn't have even a single win. "Of course you can't have a nice day. You're Lyra. You don't deserve to be loved or to have a nice day."

She fell into another coughing fit and cried until her eyes could produce no more tears and her nose, no more mucus. Her body was wrecked. She fell asleep in a pool of despair, but her dreams continued to haunt her.

CHAPTER 10

WHAT IS HOPE?

———

Lyra woke on Friday morning at 2am. She felt sick from yesterday, and she was probably not in any position to go to work on Saturday either. She would tell Lucy tomorrow that she needed an extension on her sick days. At any rate she was glad that she had the foresight to take the two days off. And hopefully she would recover.

But hope seemed out of reach. She thought about the past few days and how some of the voices seemed to give her a false sense of confidence and hope. Now all that was gone, and she needed something more.

"A release," she murmured. Her voice sounded scratchy and almost gone. It hurt to speak at all. She realized her head was pulsing. "You really shouldn't cry so much. It's bad for your health." The sound of even her own voice in her head made her angry.

"Shut up, I can cry however long I want. I'm an adult."

She didn't feel like an adult, or a person really. She wasn't particularly good with finances, and her job barely supported her. She was a problem to her own family. She hurt everyone around her. She felt like a black hole that sucked joy and positive emotions from those in its vicinity.

Lyra took some ibuprofen and chugged some water. And then she grabbed a cold piece of pizza and went back to bed.

I walk down the path.

It's not crowded with trees like everything else.

Lyra grabbed her phone, which was dead and had a crack on its screen. She cringed at the memory of her throw last night. "This is why you can't have nice things, Lyra. See what you did? You broke your own damn phone." She remembered she needed to put the TV back upright, too.

It waits for me.

The sky is blue and holds the clouds for me, showing me all kinds of pictures.

"Interesting," Lyra whispered.

I felt like I was flying as I cocked my head to the side.

It felt nice to be free.

Lyra wondered what that felt like. Freedom. "You're not allowed to go out. Remember what happened just this last time? Jesus, Lyra, you're the worst."

She felt hopeless when it came to the voices. No matter

how she managed them, they always came back. She had to pretend that she was okay, walking two paths of emotional expression. What she was feeling internally usually had to be suppressed at the risk of being disciplined for ruining the moment for others. She resented being taught this suppression in her classes, because her needs weren't being met and her feelings were largely invalidated. She was stuck. She hadn't been able to move out as a minor. She had no means or reasonable plans to run away. She had just wanted to break out of her parent's roof so that she could not have to expend energy on keeping up a façade. Her mind put on a slideshow of times where she wasn't as trained in emotional suppression and was disciplined for not being a good enough actress. She had to build another layer of ice in her armor so when her parents were yelling, she could shut down all emotions, stay still, and only speak when they requested it. In her mind she could scream and yell at them. But on the outside, a blank stare met their gaze and actively listened to see what they needed her to say to get them off her back. She was and had always been trapped.

Sadness threatened to snuff her out. "I really messed up. I always mess up. If I could just exist without having to worry about food or survival, I'd live that life. But I doubt I'll ever have that opportunity."

"Lyra, do you want people to accept you as you? Or do you want them to like you? People could never truly like you the way you exist."

Lyra pulled her legs into her chest. "I just want to be free," she murmured into her knees.

"But you can't be free. You'll never be free as long as you live, at least."

Trapped.

If only I could feel like this every day.

I breathe the freedom in.

Lyra sighed. "What am I going to do for the next ten years? Fifteen?"

"You're so stupid, you don't even know what you want to be when you grow up. And you're already in your twenties. People you went to school with are having kids, for fuck's sake. So that must mean you can't grow up. Ever."

"Maybe I should go to another city."

"And live where? Moving is expensive unless you decide to live out of your jeep. Where are you going to put all of your books? Things are going to get really cramped, and your health will decline, and you'll just be the biggest loser to come out of Hot Springs. But I'd doubt you'd succeed at leaving in the first place."

She tightened her arms around her legs. "I don't think I want to be a business partner to Lucy anymore. She's just going to fire me eventually. And then I won't be able to live by myself. Mom and Dad won't tolerate my being jobless. They are never happy when I'm not contributing to the family."

"What's the point in living anymore?" She said this last part aloud.

I wish there were someone I could share it with.

I look behind me.

Nobody.

A single tear slid down her cheek. "Nobody supports

me. Nobody will love me for just being me."

Typical.

What was I thinking?

I'm alone.

The voice and her voice merged into one. Lyra searched for peaceful ways to die in her phone. The first result in her search was the national suicide prevention lifeline number. If technology were any smarter, the lifeline people would call her.

"What am I doing?" She thought about her mom and dad; they might do a welfare check on her. They would discover her body and probably sigh from disappointment and relief. Lyra focused on the relief. "You'd no longer be a burden to them, your brother, Lucy, or any of the Destinys out there that you possibly could have hurt." Lucy's secret affair would also go down with her. Nobody would have to make sure she was fed and clothed. Nobody would have to release her from an inpatient facility. Nobody would have to feel sorry for her living and breathing. Or her mental diagnosis. Or the fact that she was incurable.

She continued her search. "It's my time. I've been a burden long enough. I'm just prolonging the inevitable. It would be nice for everyone not to have to worry about me. And I get to exist without needing anything from anyone. Maybe I should do it in the woods so that the animals can feed off my body and so that mom and dad won't have to bury me. I'll just be gone."

Just do it already.

The voice was instantly familiar. It was her mother's.

Lyra was filled with shock, and then a wave of sadness followed. A sob tore through her as she tried to fold herself inwards. She ran through possible methods of suicide: gun, knife, overdose, jump, hanging, poisoning, or medical assist. The last one felt impossible but the most desirable. Lyra wished so hard that she could walk to the inpatient facility and just let them take her life away. That way it would be painless and probably comfy.

You're taking too long.

"You're taking too long!" she retorted to her mother. She thought about all the times her mother failed at being her mother. Like the time Lyra was forgotten at church. The rest of the family had already settled in back at home before receiving a phone call from the Pastor that he had Lyra in his possession. Totally forgotten. Just like when her mother was hours late for picking Lyra up from high school. She had been incredibly frustrated and had wished she could just drive herself home. She needed to complete the lengthy list of assignments, and wasting time meant more anxiety. She always needed her mother to some degree…but her mother had never truly needed her. Nor did she seem to want her.

Ungrateful child.

"Go. Away," Lyra growled. She glanced at her clock and saw that somehow it was already 8am. She quickly pulled on a pair of pants and slid into her boots. She decided it would have to be a gun. Quick. Efficient. And it would probably silence all the voices in her head. Especially her mother's.

CHAPTER 11:

PEOPLE

Lyra was filled with anxiety of getting caught. What if she couldn't get a gun? Not taking enough pills or the torture of waiting for the pills to take effect would just leave her vulnerable to even more anxiety. She wanted it to be quick. She wanted silence without fear of having to go to work and deal with Lucy or the failure of a suicide attempt. Her mental status didn't particularly prevent her from buying a gun, but since she had never wanted one and never hunted, she would have to go get one now.

She went down to a hunting goods store and bought the cheapest gun she could find and one pack of bullets. They really didn't even ask much about her intent with the gun. Lyra assumed they were just happy to make the sale for the numbers.

It was still Friday morning. She figured she would tell Lucy that she'd like to go to church on Sunday and then kill herself this evening. Lucy had a spare key to her place, so she would be likely to find her body. Or maybe she would tell her parents she loved them and ask to have dinner at her place on Sunday. Maybe she would do both so that they could all support each other when they found her body. Or maybe Lucy would fire her over text on Saturday and then discover her body on Sunday.

Lyra pulled back into the driveway of her house and looked at it, taking it in for the last time.

People are the most complicated thing I study.

Lyra tipped her chin up towards the sky. This voice sounded philosophical.

They fight, they bring peace, and then they do it all over again.

Exhausted and resigned, Lyra listened.

I'm in a world of depression and sadness.

I give up living every day.

Lyra related to the hopelessness. She allowed self- disappointment to sink in as she realized the truth of how much she gave up on herself and her life.

Life has to win every day, no matter how close it is.

Lyra startled. "Life has to win every day." Death would be the victor of this day if she let it. Was it worth it? Did she have no inkling of desire to live with this mental illness? With the voices? No matter how nice some of the voices were?

Death only has to win once.

She tipped her head back and looked at her house. "Sometimes the pain is too much," she replied.

She pulled up her phone and looked to see if there were any facilities that would do assisted suicides. She quickly found that Arkansas banned the Death with Dignity Act. "Of course they did." She rolled her eyes, remembering the lesson in church where the teacher told them all that people who die of suicide go to Hell. She was already in Hell. It would probably feel like home.

Anyway, she didn't think mentally ill patients like herself would qualify for such a thing even if Arkansas offered it. Arkansas seemed to treat their mentally ill population very poorly, preferring prison sentences over the help they so desperately need. The few facilities that were designed to help were limited to begin with. Lyra was lucky that her behavior had only led her to inpatient care and not prison walls. But those facilities—and her life—were a prison of their own.

She placed the gun on the dashboard and regarded it. "It's you or me. And I'm thinking I don't want to die…because I'm talking to a gun instead of letting it do the talking."

"Maybe we need to check into an inpatient facility and get some help. We don't want to die just yet."

Lyra's eyes filled with tears as she listened to this voice. Her voice. She suddenly didn't want to die. In spite of all of the mental pain she's been through these past few days, she didn't want to end it just yet. She would never hear the birds again. Taste another warm bagel. Smell the honeysuckles. Or buy some lilies.

"But we did all this work…"

She stared down the gun."It's okay to quit sometimes. And ask for help."

Lyra sighed and picked up her phone.

CHAPTER 12

DOCTORS

———

There was a steady stream of people in and out of her room while she just laid in bed, looking out the window into the evening. It was a beautiful sunset, but she still felt strongly like she wanted to die with it.

"Life can be better if you want to work things out with it," the doctor said gently.

Lyra shook her head softly. "I have schizophrenia…I don't think I could, unless the voices go away."

"We just need to get you back on your treatments. You can get better." He held her gaze. "But you have to keep taking the medicine."

"I hate taking medicine."

"I know. How about as a start, I can see you regularly

for talk therapy?"

"Not sure what good that will do," Lyra shrugged. "Talk therapy can be beneficial if you actively participate."

Lyra gave her doctor the silent treatment. She wasn't sure why she had decided to come here when she was so determined to die.

"Doc…can you imagine having an incurable disease for the majority of your life? And no God out there will heed your cries for help? And doctors are always telling you that they can ease your pain, but not take it away fully?"

The doctor maintained his professional listening pose as he glanced from her to his chart.

"I guess not." She murmured as she continued to look out the window again.

The doctor gave her arm a light squeeze, and with a small smile that she assumed was meant to be encouraging and not morbid, he handed her off to a nurse while he went to write up some notes. One nurse was left behind to stand guard and make sure that Lyra wouldn't hurt herself.

CHAPTER 13

SEMICOLON

Lyra scribbled in her new notebook aimlessly. Every once in awhile, she would write something down in regard to her thoughts. Occasionally she would even start planning some things to do when she was back home. Every time she opened to a blank page, she would circle back to when the doctor walked in with an armful of gifts. She was really nervous about the attention she was getting and had awkwardly accepted the gifts and read the note before placing the flowers down and returning to her bed. A lovely bouquet of lilies, now sitting on a cabinet with the balloons tied around the vase. She gazed at them for a second.

"Those lovely lilies," she murmured to herself. "How can you sit there so beautiful

When there is so much dread? They look so peaceful. Lovely lilies, what's your secret? Tell me so."

Lyra briefly smiled at the voice as she copied these words down in her notebook.

APPENDIX OF SUICIDE HOTLINES AND HELP

A

ALGERIA

SUICIDE PREVENTION RESOURCES

Emergency: 34342 and 43

Suicide Hotline: 0021 3983 2000 58

ARGENTINA

SUICIDE PREVENTION RESOURCES

National Emergency Number: 911

Centro de Asistencia al Suicida
In the greater Buenos Aires area, dial: 135
Otherwise, call: 5275-1135 or 0800 345 1435

ARMENIA

SUICIDE PREVENTION RESOURCES

Emergency: 911 and 112

Suicide Hotline: (2) 538194

AUSTRALIA

SUICIDE PREVENTION RESOURCES

National Emergency Number: 000

Lifeline Australia
24/7 crisis support, dial: 13 11 14
12pm–12am AEDT, text: 0477 13 11 14

AUSTRIA

SUICIDE PREVENTION RESOURCES

National Emergency Numbers, dial:
Police: 133 · Ambulance: 144 · Fire Brigade: 122

Telefon Seelsorge 24/7 crisis support, dial: 142

Rat auf Draht 24/7 (Youth): 147

For online chat support, visit Telefon Seelsorge's website;
available from 5pm–10pm Central European Time

B

BAHAMAS

SUICIDE PREVENTION RESOURCES

Emergency: 911

Suicide Hotline: (2) 322-2763

BAHRAIN

SUICIDE PREVENTION RESOURCES

Emergency: 999

BANGLADESH

SUICIDE PREVENTION RESOURCES

Emergency: 999

BARBADOS

SUICIDE PREVENTION RESOURCES

Emergency: 911

Samaritan Barbados Suicide Hotline: (246) 4299999

BELGIUM

SUICIDE PREVENTION RESOURCES

National Emergency Number: 112 Zelfmoord

24/7 crisis support, dial: 1813

For online chat support, visit Zelfmoord's website; available from 6:30pm–10pm Central European Time

BOLIVIA

SUICIDE PREVENTION RESOURCES

Emergency: 911

Suicide Hotline: 3911270

BOSNIA & HERZEGOVINA

SUICIDE PREVENTION RESOURCES

Suicide Hotline: 080 05 03 05

BOTSWANA

SUICIDE PREVENTION RESOURCES

Emergency: 911

Suicide Hotline: +2673911270

BRAZIL

SUICIDE PREVENTION RESOURCES

Emergency: 188

BULGARIA

SUICIDE PREVENTION RESOURCES

Emergency: 112

Suicide Hotline: 0035 9249 17 223

C

CANADA

SUICIDE PREVENTION RESOURCES

National Emergency Number: 911

Crisis Services Canada
24/7 crisis support, dial: 1-833-456-4566
In Quebec, dial: 1-866-APPELLE (277-3553)
Crisis Text Line 24/7 text support, text: HOME to 741741
Text Support 4pm–12am ET, text: 45645

CHINA

SUICIDE PREVENTION RESOURCES

Emergency: 110

Suicide Hotline: 800-810-1117

CHILE

SUICIDE PREVENTION RESOURCES

National Emergency Numbers, call:
Police: 133 · Medical Assistance: 131

Teléfono de la Esperanza, dial: (00 56 42) 22 12 00

COLOMBIA

SUICIDE PREVENTION RESOURCES

National emergency number: 123
Teléfono de la esperanza, dial: (57-1) 372 24 25

Ministerio de Salud y Protección Social (Ministry of

Health and Social Protection)
Visit the website for region-specific suicide hotlines

CROATIA

SUICIDE PREVENTION RESOURCES

Emergency: 112

CYPRUS

SUICIDE PREVENTION RESOURCES

Emergency: 112

Suicide Hotline: 8000 7773

CZECH REPUBLIC

SUICIDE PREVENTION RESOURCES

Emergency: 112

D

DENMARK

SUICIDE PREVENTION RESOURCES

National Emergency Number: 112

Helpline: 1813

24/7 crisis support, dial: 1813

E

EGYPT

SUICIDE PREVENTION RESOURCES

Emergency: 122

ESTONIA

SUICIDE PREVENTION RESOURCES

Emergency: 112

Suicide Hotline: 3726558088

Suicide Hotline in Russian: 3726555688

ETHIOPIA

SUICIDE PREVENTION RESOURCES

Emergency: 911

F

FINLAND

SUICIDE PREVENTION RESOURCES

Emergency: 112

Suicide Hotline: 010 195 202

FRANCE

SUICIDE PREVENTION RESOURCES

National Emergency Number: 112

Suicide Écoute 24/7 crisis support, dial: 01 45 39 40 00

SOS Suicide Phénix 1pm–11pm CET, dial: 01 40 44 46 45

G

GERMANY

SUICIDE PREVENTION RESOURCES

National Emergency Number: 112

Telefon Seelsorge 24/7 crisis support, dial: 0800 111 0 111
For chat or email support, visit TelefonSeelsorge's website
Suicide Hotline: 08001810771

GHANA

SUICIDE PREVENTION RESOURCES

Emergency: 999

Suicide Hotline: 2332 444 71279

GREECE

SUICIDE PREVENTION RESOURCES

Emergency: 1018

GUYANA

SUICIDE PREVENTION RESOURCES

Emergency: 999

Suicide Hotline: 223-0001

H

HOLLAND

SUICIDE PREVENTION RESOURCES

Suicide Hotline: 09000767

HONG KONG

SUICIDE PREVENTION RESOURCES

National Emergency Number: 999

The Samaritans 24/7 crisis support, dial: 2896 0000

HUNGARY

SUICIDE PREVENTION RESOURCES

Suicide Hotline: 116123

I

IRELAND

SUICIDE PREVENTION RESOURCES

National emergency number: 112 or 999

The Samaritans 24/7 mental health support, dial: 116123

Mental Health Ireland
Crisis Text Line 24/7 text support, text: HOME to 50808
Suicide Hotline: +4408457909090

INDIA

SUICIDE PREVENTION RESOURCES

Suicide Hotline: 8888817666

INDONESIA

SUICIDE PREVENTION RESOURCES

Emergency: 112

Suicide Hotline: 1-800-273-8255

IRAN

SUICIDE PREVENTION RESOURCES

Emergency: 110

Suicide Hotline: 1480

ISRAEL

SUICIDE PREVENTION RESOURCES

Emergency: 100

Suicide Hotline: 1201

ITALY

SUICIDE PREVENTION RESOURCES

Emergency: 112

Suicide Hotline: 800860022

J

JAMAICA

SUICIDE PREVENTION RESOURCES

Suicide Hotline: 1-888-429-KARE (5273)

JAPAN

SUICIDE PREVENTION RESOURCES

Emergency: 110

Suicide Hotline: 810352869090

JORDAN

SUICIDE PREVENTION RESOURCES

Emergency: 911

Suicide Hotline: 110

K

KENYA

SUICIDE PREVENTION RESOURCES

Emergency: 999

Suicide Hotline: '722178177

KUWAIT

SUICIDE PREVENTION RESOURCES

Emergency 112

Suicide Hotline: 94069304

L

LATVIA

SUICIDE PREVENTION RESOURCES

Emergency: 113

Suicide Hotline: 371 67222922

LEBANON

SUICIDE PREVENTION RESOURCES

Suicide Hotline: 1564

LIBERIA

SUICIDE PREVENTION RESOURCES

Emergency: 911

Suicide Hotline: 6534308

LUXEMBOURG

SUICIDE PREVENTION RESOURCES

Emergency: 112

Suicide Hotline: 352 45 45 45

MALAYSIA

SUICIDE PREVENTION RESOURCES

Emergency: 999

Suicide Hotline: (06) 2842500

MALTA

SUICIDE PREVENTION RESOURCES

Suicide Hotline: 179

MAURITIUS

SUICIDE PREVENTION RESOURCES

Emergency: 112

Suicide Hotline: +230 800 93 93

MEXICO

SUICIDE PREVENTION RESOURCES

National emergency number: 911

Consejo Ciudadano 24/7 crisis support, dial: 55 5533-5533

Suicide Hotline: 5255102550

N

NETHERLANDS

SUICIDE PREVENTION RESOURCES

Emergency: 112

Suicide Hotline: 900 0113

NEW ZEALAND

SUICIDE PREVENTION RESOURCES

National Emergency Number: 111

Lifeline Aotearoa
24/7 crisis support, dial: 0800 LIFELINE (0800 543 354)
24/7 text support, text: HELP to 4357

Suicide Hotline: 1737

NIGERIA

SUICIDE PREVENTION RESOURCES

Suicide Hotline: 234 8092106493

NORWAY

SUICIDE PREVENTION RESOURCES

Emergency: 112

Suicide Hotline: +4781533300

P

PAKISTAN

SUICIDE PREVENTION RESOURCES

Emergency: 115

PHILIPPINES

SUICIDE PREVENTION RESOURCES

Emergency: 911

Suicide Hotline: 028969191

POLAND

SUICIDE PREVENTION RESOURCES

Emergency: 112

Suicide Hotline: 5270000

PORTUGAL

SUICIDE PREVENTION RESOURCES

Emergency: 112

Suicide Hotlines: 21 854 07 40 and 8 96 898 21 50

Q

QATAR

SUICIDE PREVENTION RESOURCES

Emergency: 999

R

ROMANIA

SUICIDE PREVENTION RESOURCES

Emergency number: 112

Suicide Hotline: 0800 801200

RUSSIA

SUICIDE PREVENTION RESOURCES

Emergency: 112

Suicide Hotline: 0078202577577

S

SAINT VINCENT AND THE GRENADINES

Suicide Hotline: (9784) 456 1044

SAUDI ARABIA

SUICIDE PREVENTION RESOURCES

Emergency: 112

SERBIA

SUICIDE PREVENTION RESOURCES

Suicide Hotline: (+381) 21-6623-393

SINGAPORE

SUICIDE PREVENTION RESOURCES

National Emergency Number: 999 (police) or 995

The Samaritans of Singapore
24/7 crisis support, dial: 1800-221 4444
Visit The Samaritans' website for online chat support

SPAIN

SUICIDE PREVENTION RESOURCES

National emergency numbers: 112

Teléfono de la Esperanza
24/7 crisis support, dial: 717 003 717

Suicide Hotline: 914590050

SOUTH AFRICA

SUICIDE PREVENTION RESOURCES

National Emergency Numbers

Police: 10111 or Ambulance: 10177

South African Depression and Anxiety Group
24/7 crisis support, dial: 0800 567 567

Suicide Hotline: 0514445691

SOUTH KOREA

SUICIDE PREVENTION RESOURCES

Emergency: 112

Suicide Hotline: (02) 7158600

SRI LANKA

SUICIDE PREVENTION RESOURCES

Suicide Hotline: 011 057 2222662

SUDAN

SUICIDE PREVENTION RESOURCES

Suicide Hotline: (249) 11-555-253

SWEDEN

SUICIDE PREVENTION RESOURCES

National emergency number: 112

Mind Självmordslinjen 24/7 phone support, dial: 90101
In cases of acute crisis, call: 112
For online chat support, visit Självmordslinjen's website
Suicide Hotline: 46317112400

SWITZERLAND

SUICIDE PREVENTION RESOURCES

National Emergency Number: 112

Die Dargebotene Hand 24/7 mental health support, dial: 143

For online chat support between 10am–10pm, visit
Die Dargebotene Hand's website

T

TANZANIA

SUICIDE PREVENTION RESOURCES

Emergency: 112

THAILAND

SUICIDE PREVENTION RESOURCES

Suicide Hotline: (02) 713-6793

TONGA

SUICIDE PREVENTION RESOURCES

Suicide Hotline: 23000

TRINIDAD AND TOBAGO

SUICIDE PREVENTION RESOURCES

Suicide Hotline: (868) 645 2800

TUNISIA

SUICIDE PREVENTION RESOURCES

Emergency: 197

TURKEY

SUICIDE PREVENTION RESOURCES

Emergency: 112

U

UGANDA

SUICIDE PREVENTION RESOURCES

Emergency: 112

Suicide Hotline: 0800 21 21 21

UKRAINE

SUICIDE PREVENTION RESOURCES

Hotline Face to Face: 0487 327715

Hotline Phone: 0482 226565

Hotline Emergency Number: 112

UNITED ARAB EMIRATES

SUICIDE PREVENTION RESOURCES

Suicide Hotline: 800 46342

UNITED KINGDOM

SUICIDE PREVENTION RESOURCES

National emergency number: 999 or 112

The Samaritans 24/7 mental health support, dial: 116 123

Campaign Against Living Miserably (CALM)
Crisis support 5pm–12am BST or GMT, dial: 0800 58 58 58
Crisis Text Line 24/7 text support, text: HOME to 85258

Suicide Hotline: 0800 689 5652

UNITED STATES

SUICIDE PREVENTION RESOURCES

Emergency: 911

Suicide Hotline: (800) 273-8255
You may also call, text, or chat: 988

Childhelp National Child Abuse Hotline
Call or text: 1-800-422-4453
For issues related to child abuse, Childhelp
connects you with a professional counselors to help

in a crisis, and provide information on how to get help. They offer phone support in 170 languages, or you can chat online with a counselor.

Crisis Text Line
Text "HOME" to 741741 · crisistextline.org
Crisis Text Line provides free emotional support and information to teens in any type of crisis, including feeling suicidal. You can text with a trained specialist 24 hours a day.

You can also text 741741 in the US or UK (686868 in Canada), reach out via WhatsApp or message Crisis Text Line on Facebook for help. You'll be matched with a volunteer counselor, who is supervised by a licensed, trained mental health professional.

HOT SPRINGS ARKANSAS SUICIDE HOTLINES

Community Counseling Services
24 Hour Emergency Phone
(501) 624-7111
1-800-264-2410

A FEW OTHER LGBTQIA HELPLINES THAT OFFER SUPPORT, BUT NOT NECESSARILY CRISIS INTERVENTION

LGBT National Hotline: 1-888-843-4564

LGBT National Youth Talkline: 1-800-246-7743

LGBT Senior Hotline: 1-888-234-7243

SAMHSA National Helpline: 1-800-662-4357
If you are struggling with addiction or are concerned about a loved one's alcohol or drug abuse, you can contact the hotline for the Substance Abuse and Mental Health Services Administration. This US government agency offers

support and information about treatment and recovery.
National Deaf Domestic Violence Hotline: 1-855-812-1001
The National Deaf Domestic Violence Hotline is a spinoff
from the NDVH specifically for Deaf and Hard of Hearing
individuals. You can get help over email, or talk via video
call to a trained counselor.

National Domestic Violence Hotline
Text "START" to 88788 or call 1-800-799-7233
Anyone who is experiencing domestic violence and/or
abuse, plus anyone concerned about a friend, family
member or loved one can call the National Domestic
Violence Hotline 24 hours a day, seven days a week.
They offer support in more than 200 languages,
and offer a confidential, secure online chat.
RAINN: 1-800-656-4673
The Rape, Abuse & Incest National Network's hotline
is for anyone who's experienced sexual abuse or assault.
When you call its main hotline, you'll be connected with
someone at a local organization in your area who can
provide live support and direct you to additional resources.
RAINN also offers live chat on its website.

Society for the Prevention of Teen Suicide
Teen Section: sptsusa.org/teens/
This website has a teen section where you can find
information to help yourself or a friend who may be
having suicidal thoughts. You can also find information
on how to cope if a friend dies by suicide.

Suicide Prevention Resource Center
Web: sprc.org | E-mail: info@sprc.org
Phone: 877-GET-SPRC (438–7772)

Trans Lifeline: 1-877-565-8860
The Trans Lifeline provides support specifically for
transgender and questioning callers, run trans people.

They provide support during a crisis and can also offer guidance to anyone who is questioning their gender and needs support. The hotline is available between 7 a.m. and 1 a.m. PST (9 a.m. to 3 a.m. CST or 10 a.m. to 4 a.m. EST). But operators are often available during off-hours, so no matter when you need to call, you should.

Trevor Project
thetrevorproject.org
The Trevor Project provides suicide prevention and crisis intervention services to lesbian, gay, bisexual, transgender, and questioning (LGBTQ) young people. It offers free, 24/7, confidential counseling through the following: Trevor Lifeline— toll-free phone line at 1-866-488-7386; TrevorText—text START to 678-678; TrevorChat—instant messaging at TheTrevorProject.org/Help. It also runs TrevorSpace, an affirming social networking site for LGBTQ youth at TrevorSpace.org.

Veterans Crisis Line (800) 273-8255, PRESS 1
Text 838255
You may also call, text, or chat: 988

We Are The 22:
855-932-7384
This is a veteran suicide prevention resource that is for Arkansas Veteran Residents only.
YouthLine
Text: teen2teen to 839863
Call: 1-877-968-8491
YouthLine provides a safe space for children and adults ages 11 to 21, to talk through any issues they may be facing, including eating disorders, relationship or family concerns, bullying, sexual identity, depression, self-harm, anxiety and thoughts of suicide.

Z

ZAMBIA

SUICIDE PREVENTION RESOURCES

Emergency: 999

Suicide Hotline: +260960264040

ZIMBABWE

SUICIDE PREVENTION RESOURCES

Emergency: 999

Suicide Hotline: 080 12 333 333

ABOUT THE AUTHOR

Emily Franchini is a poet, novelist, and mental health advocate. She began writing at an early age and won the Poetry.com Editor's Choice Award in 2008 when she was fifteen years old for her poem The Wind. Partially inspired by her own wellness journey, her debut novella, Lyra, works to inspire more mental health awareness and empower the mental health community. She plans to use its profits to assist the under- financed mental health organizations in her home state of Arkansas, where she now lives with her husband Brian and their shepherd husky mix dog Oakley (AKA Oakley-Dokely), chunky tabby cat Tim (AKA Timmy, Tomothy, TIMAEEEY, and Chunk), and their senior cat Jasmine (AKA Jazz, Pretty Girl, and Siren).